Anytime, Anywhere

Anytime,

Anywhere

a little boy's prayer

by Marcus Hummon
art by Steve Johnson and Lou Fancher

Atheneum Books for young Readers
New york London Toronto Sydney

Atheneum Books for Young Readers
An imprint of Simon & Schuster Children's Publishing Division
1230 Avenue of the Americas
New York, New York 10020

Book design by Lou Fancher
The text for this book is set in Cantoria MT.
The illustrations for this book are rendered in collage and acrylic on paper.
Manufactured in China
2 4 6 8 10 9 7 5 3
Library of Congress Cataloging-in-Publication Data
Hummon, Marcus.
Anytime, anywhere: a little boy's prayer/Marcus Hummon ; illustrated by
Steve Johnson and Lou Fancher.—1st ed.
p.   cm.
Summary: As he prays one night for everything from the tiniest ladybug to the
mailman with a broken leg, Isaac asks his weary father about such things as
whether everyone prays to the same god and how a bedtime prayer can be
said by someone who has no bed.
ISBN-13: 978-1-4169-4856-8
ISBN-10: 1-4169-4856-2
[1. Prayer—Fiction. 2. Bedtime—Fiction. 3. Fathers and sons—Fiction.
4. Compassion—Fiction.] I. Johnson, Steve, 1960– ill. II. Fancher, Lou, ill.
III. Title.
PZ7.H8916Any 2009
[E]–dc22   2007048189

This book is dedicated
to Caney, whose prayers
started it all.
—M. H.

For young hearts
open to faith
—S. J. and L. F.

"The end," said Daddy, shutting our bedtime book with a snap.

I asked for one more book.

"Two books. You know the rules," he said with a smile. "Time for your prayers, Isaac."

I knew the rules. "Okay, Daddy."

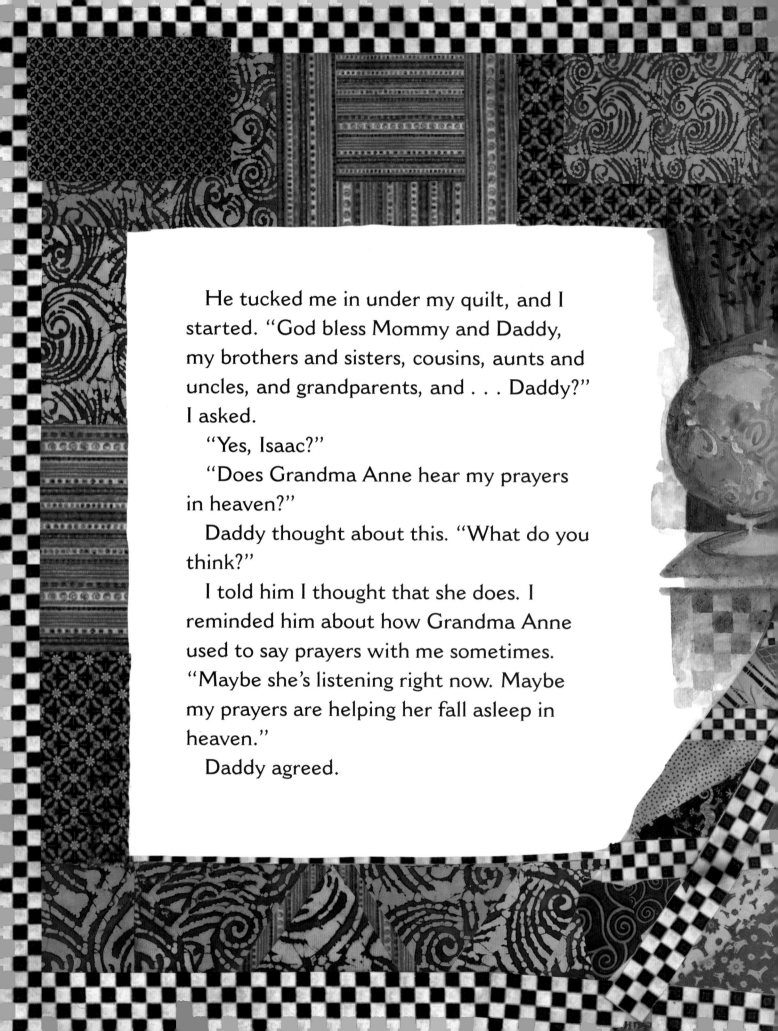

He tucked me in under my quilt, and I started. "God bless Mommy and Daddy, my brothers and sisters, cousins, aunts and uncles, and grandparents, and . . . Daddy?" I asked.

"Yes, Isaac?"

"Does Grandma Anne hear my prayers in heaven?"

Daddy thought about this. "What do you think?"

I told him I thought that she does. I reminded him about how Grandma Anne used to say prayers with me sometimes. "Maybe she's listening right now. Maybe my prayers are helping her fall asleep in heaven."

Daddy agreed.

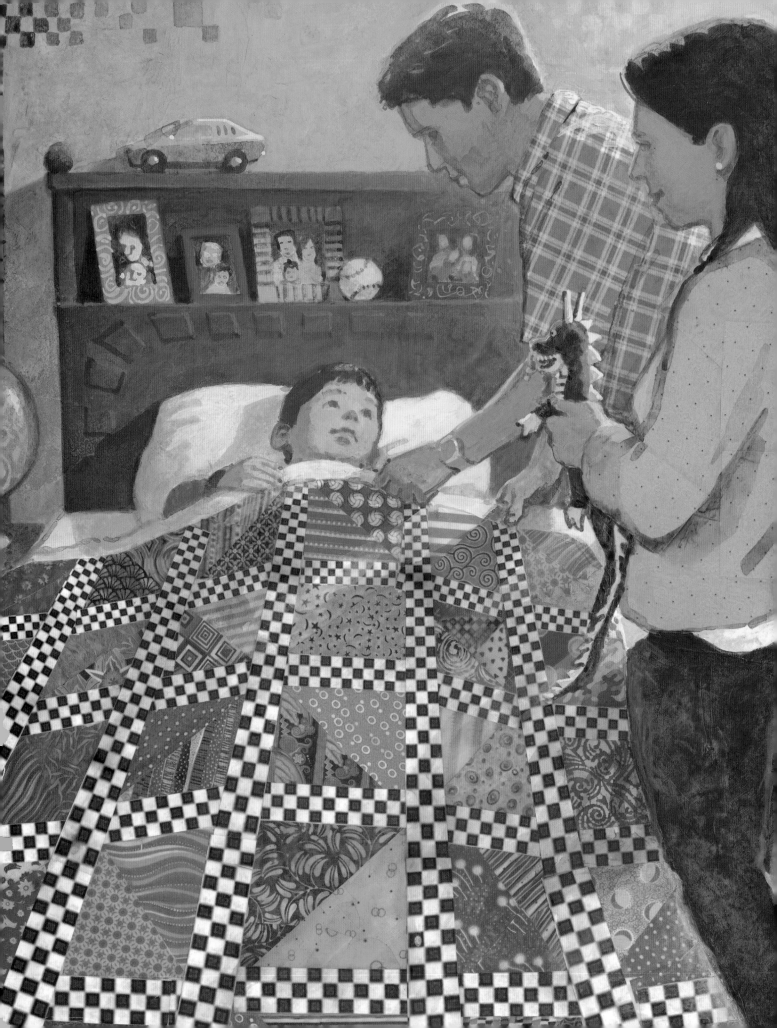

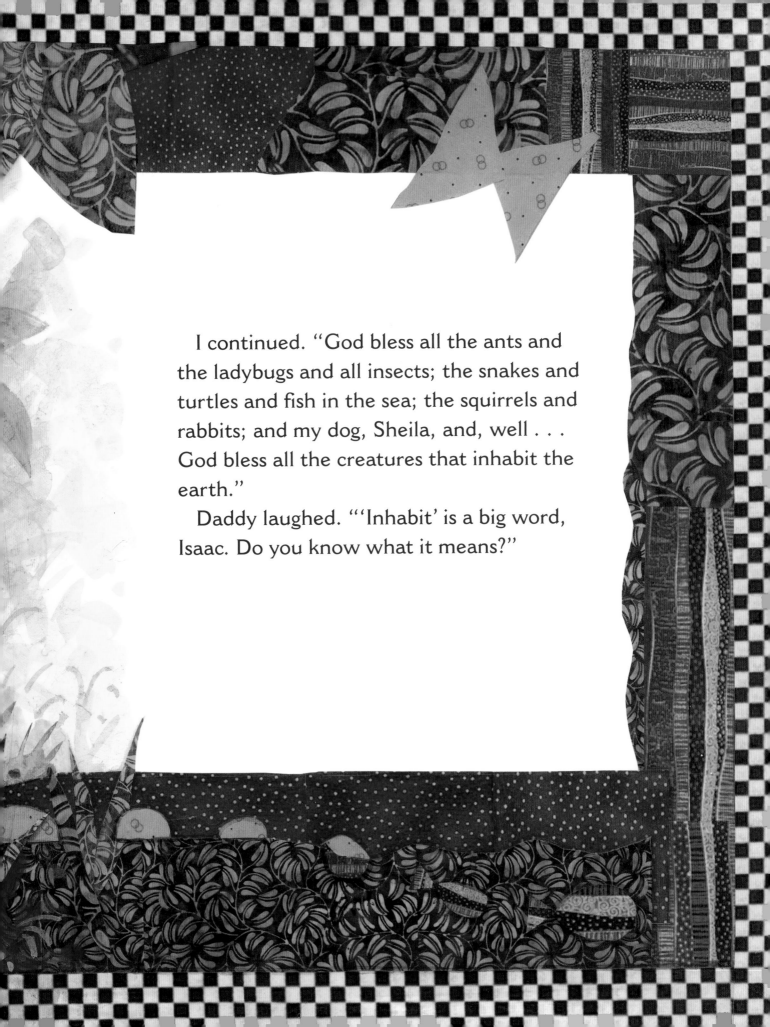

I continued. "God bless all the ants and the ladybugs and all insects; the snakes and turtles and fish in the sea; the squirrels and rabbits; and my dog, Sheila, and, well . . . God bless all the creatures that inhabit the earth."

Daddy laughed. "'Inhabit' is a big word, Isaac. Do you know what it means?"

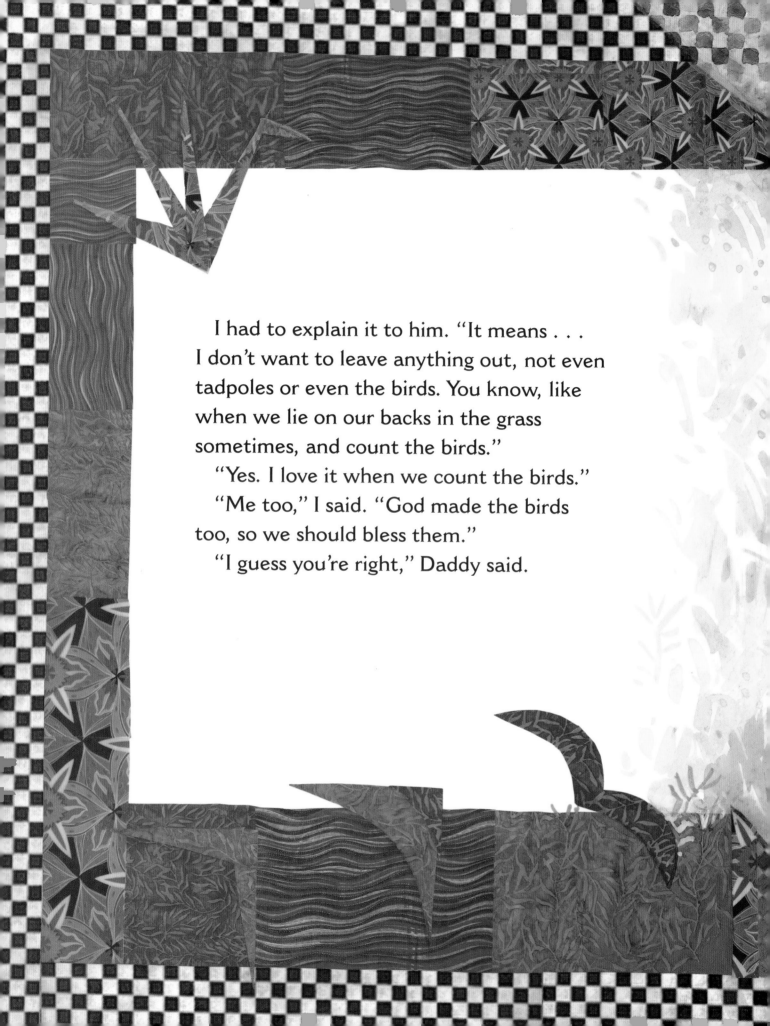

I had to explain it to him. "It means . . .
I don't want to leave anything out, not even
tadpoles or even the birds. You know, like
when we lie on our backs in the grass
sometimes, and count the birds."

"Yes. I love it when we count the birds."

"Me too," I said. "God made the birds
too, so we should bless them."

"I guess you're right," Daddy said.

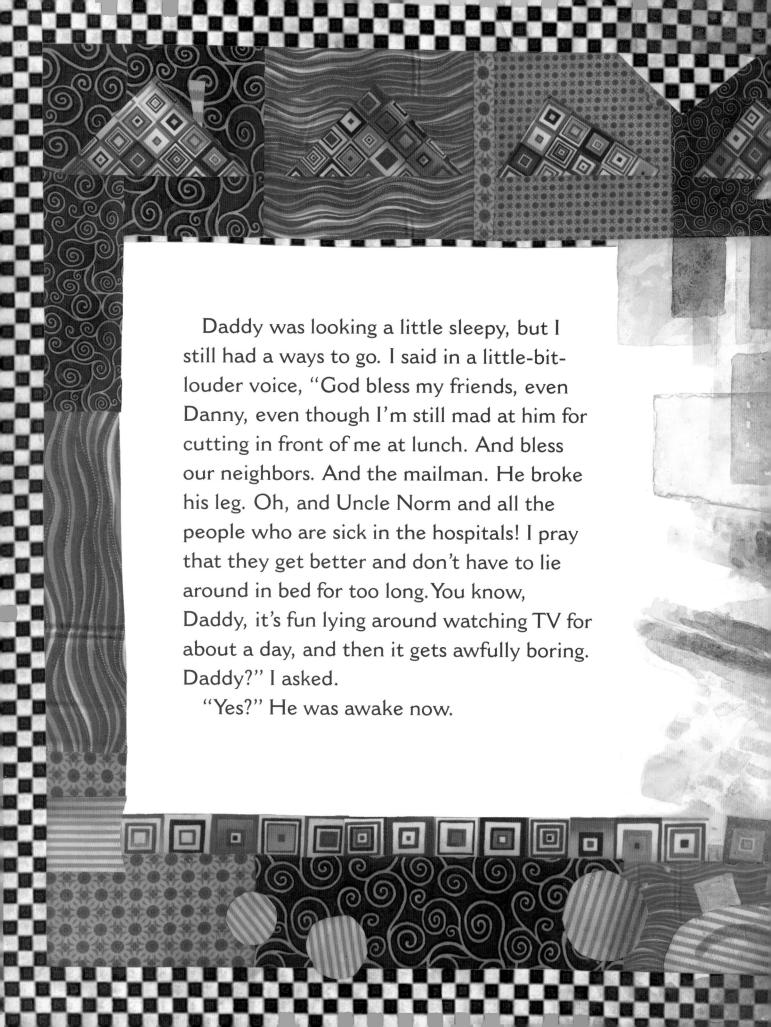

Daddy was looking a little sleepy, but I still had a ways to go. I said in a little-bit-louder voice, "God bless my friends, even Danny, even though I'm still mad at him for cutting in front of me at lunch. And bless our neighbors. And the mailman. He broke his leg. Oh, and Uncle Norm and all the people who are sick in the hospitals! I pray that they get better and don't have to lie around in bed for too long. You know, Daddy, it's fun lying around watching TV for about a day, and then it gets awfully boring. Daddy?" I asked.

"Yes?" He was awake now.

"Do you remember when I was sick?
Did you pray for me?"
"I always pray for you, Isaac," he said.
I told him that must be how come I got better.

"And Daddy?" I asked. "Should I pray for people in jail?"

Daddy kind of scrunched his eyebrows at this. "That's a new one, Isaac. What made you think about people in jail?"

"I wore my black-and-white shirt today and Danny said I looked like a jailbird. So I started thinking, it must be lonely in jail." Daddy agreed. "Have you ever been in jail?" I asked him.

He said, "Nope."

"If you ever have to go to jail, I'll pray for you."

Daddy thanked me for that and said, "Anything else?"

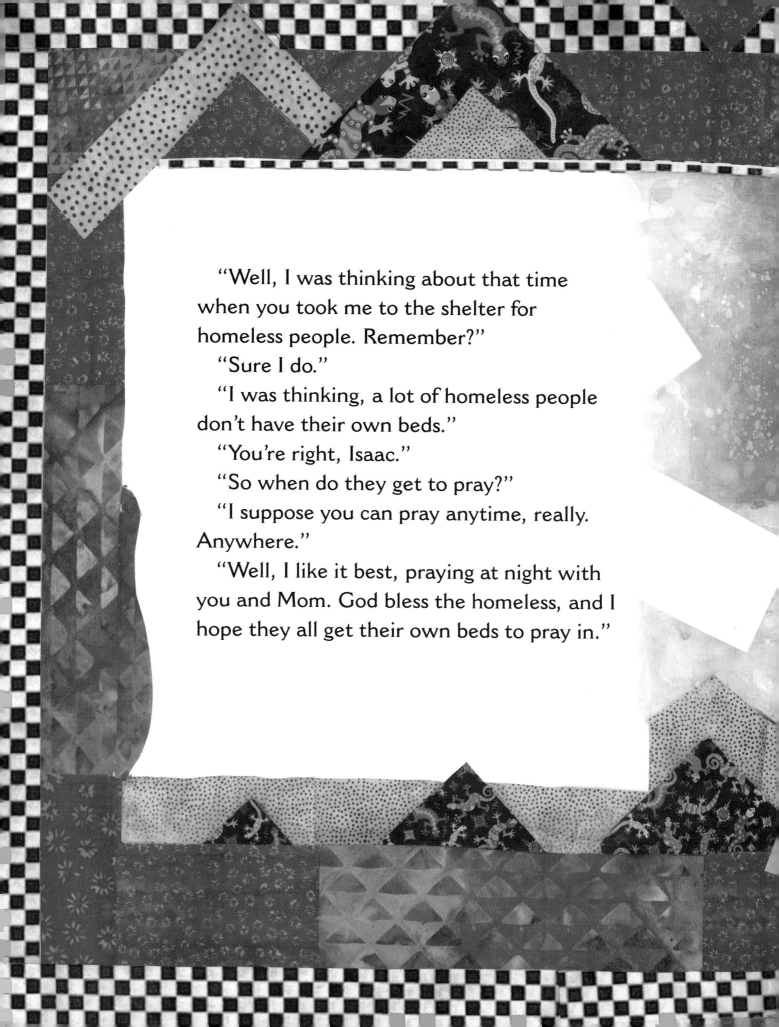

"Well, I was thinking about that time when you took me to the shelter for homeless people. Remember?"

"Sure I do."

"I was thinking, a lot of homeless people don't have their own beds."

"You're right, Isaac."

"So when do they get to pray?"

"I suppose you can pray anytime, really. Anywhere."

"Well, I like it best, praying at night with you and Mom. God bless the homeless, and I hope they all get their own beds to pray in."

Daddy must have thought that my prayers were done because he said, "Okay, Isaac, those were good prayers. Now give me a kiss good night."

"Wait, wait, wait. We forgot the best part," I said.

"What's that?"

"I gotta pray for world peace!"

"That's a big prayer, Isaac."

"It's a big world, Daddy."

Daddy kind of laughed when I said that, but I figured I had better hurry up and get the rest of my prayers in.

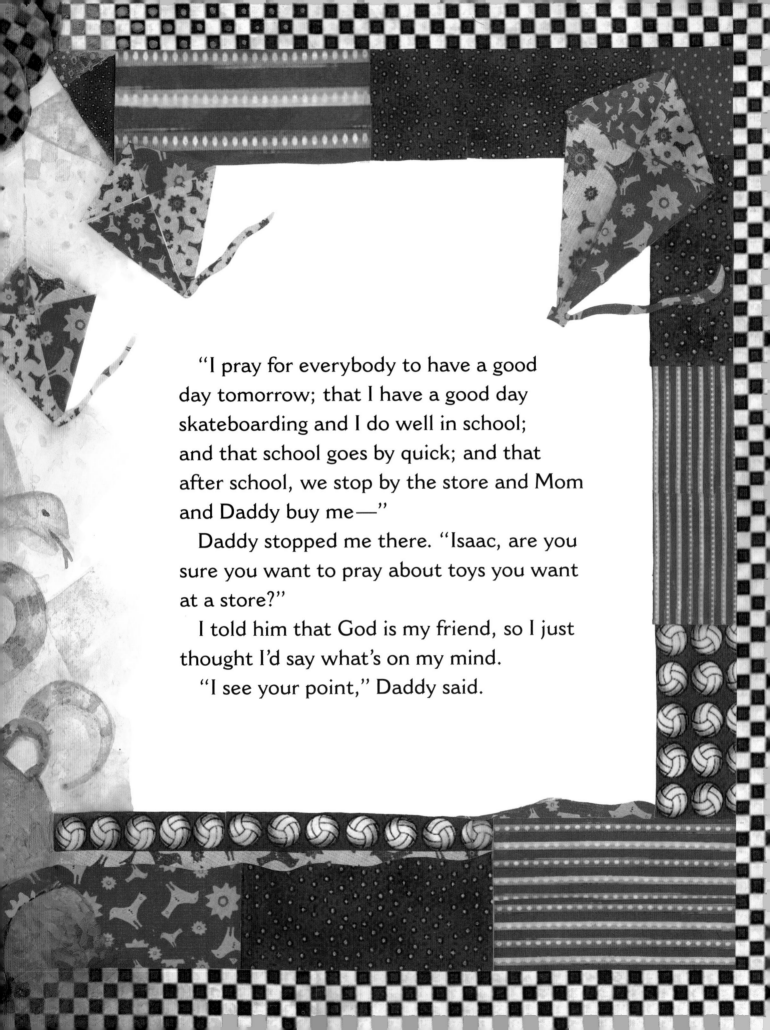

"I pray for everybody to have a good day tomorrow; that I have a good day skateboarding and I do well in school; and that school goes by quick; and that after school, we stop by the store and Mom and Daddy buy me—"

Daddy stopped me there. "Isaac, are you sure you want to pray about toys you want at a store?"

I told him that God is my friend, so I just thought I'd say what's on my mind.

"I see your point," Daddy said.

He started to get up, but I had one more question. "Does everybody pray when they go to bed?"

"A lot of people do," said Daddy.

"Do they pray to the same God as we do?"

Daddy smiled. "What do you think?"

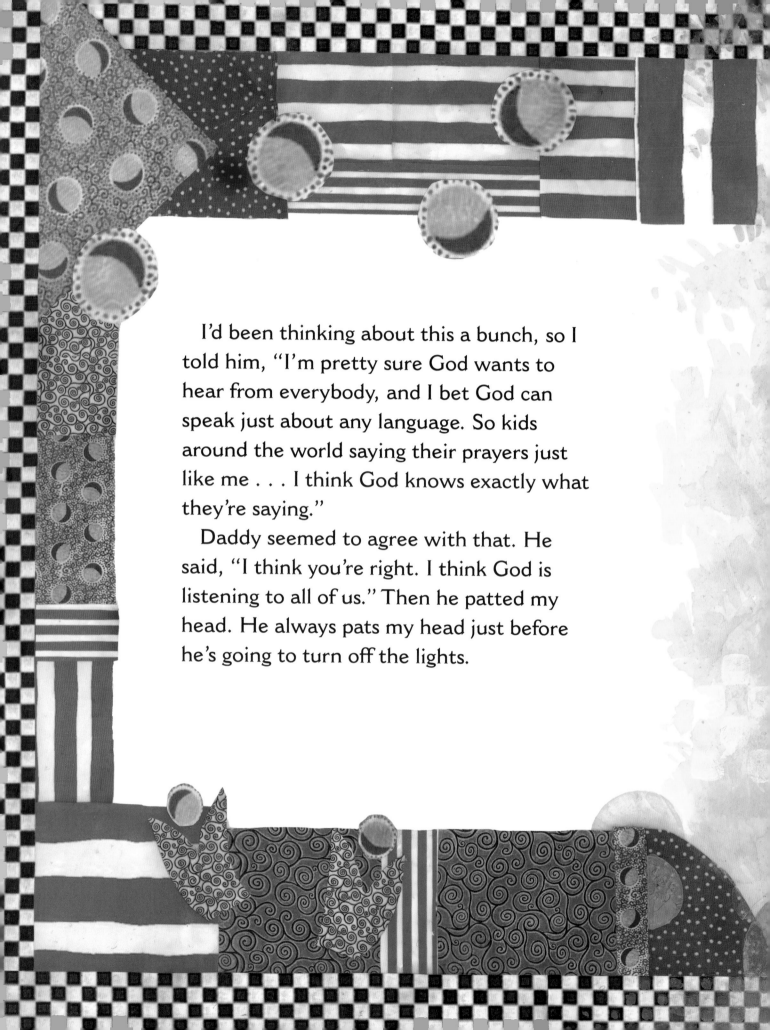

I'd been thinking about this a bunch, so I told him, "I'm pretty sure God wants to hear from everybody, and I bet God can speak just about any language. So kids around the world saying their prayers just like me . . . I think God knows exactly what they're saying."

Daddy seemed to agree with that. He said, "I think you're right. I think God is listening to all of us." Then he patted my head. He always pats my head just before he's going to turn off the lights.

"Daddy?"

"Yes, Isaac?"

"I think God loves me."

Daddy smiled big this time. "He sure does. . . . And do you know what else?"

"What?"

"I think it's time for bed," he said. But I had to sneak in one more question.

"You know how we have a rule about two books before bedtime?"

"Yeah."

"Are there any rules about how many prayers you can say?"

He kissed the top of my head. "No, Isaac, no rules about praying. You can say as many prayers as you want."

That seemed just right to me. "I love you, Daddy."

"I love you, Isaac. I'll see you in the morning."